MEGA

Make England Great Again

A play for the stage
by Francis Beckett

TSL Drama

First published in Great Britain in 2025
By TSL Drama, Rickmansworth

Copyright © 2025 Francis Beckett

ISBN: 978-1-917426-39-8

Rights of performance

Characters
in order of appearance

Max Moore, Prime Minister and leader of the Britons First Party
Samantha, a journalist
King Charles III
Pam Jones, Leader of the Opposition
Michael Jones, her husband

Running Time
Approx. 70 minutes excluding interval

Make England Great Again
was first performed at Upstairs at the
Gatehouse in Highgate Village
on 30 September 2025 with the following cast:

Max Moore ....Silas Hawkins

King Charles III ....Clive Greenwood

Samantha ....Abi Haberfield

Pam Jones ....Miranda Colmans

Michael Jones ....Clive Greenwood

Director: Owain Rose

Lighting design and operation: Tim Solomons

SCENE 1

Sounds of wild cheering, shouts of "Max" and "Maxi" and "Britons First" and "Mega, Mega, Mega, now, now, now." KING Charles III sits and listens (or watches on a screen). Ragged singing: first God Save the King, but this is overtaken by a new song:

> It's the same the whole world over
> It's the Brits what gets the blame
> It's the rest what gets the gravy
> Ain't it all a bleeding shame?
>
> (*More cheering. The* KING *rises and presses a switch; the sound ends abruptly,* MAX *enters, and the* KING *rises to meet him.*)

King:	Good morning, Prime Minister.
Max:	Your majesty.
King:	You don't have to keep calling me your majesty, you know. There's a certain informality allowed to Prime Ministers.
Max:	Right-oh. Charlie it is from now on.
King:	Sir will be quite adequate.
Max:	Right. Well. You can call me Max. Maxi if you like, though that's usually reserved for pretty girls.
King:	Prime Minister.
Max:	Whatever floats your boat. (*He sits*).
King	Perhaps we ought to maintain some of the formalities…
Max:	(*Jumping up from his chair.*) Sorry. You have to sit first.
King:	(*Sitting.*) Please sit down, Prime Minister. I hardly need ask why you're here, having heard your speech last night.
Max:	Quite.

King: I don't want to stand on my dignity, but there is a convention that the sovereign is told first if a dissolution of Parliament is required.

Max: Sorry.

King: You've only been Prime Minister for six days.

Max: I know. I know. Problem was, although mine was was the biggest single party in the House of Commons, we didn't have an overall majority. The voters slipped up there, you see.

King: I understood that enough MPs from other parties were willing to support you.

Max: They were, at first. But then, you see, because the voters made this mistake of not giving us quite enough seats, the establishment could catch us out with a procedural trick.

King: A procedural trick?

Max: Yes. They said: if you do something the majority of MPs don't like, we'll vote it down.

King: That is, arguably, the function of Parliament.

Max: They wanted to use Parliament to frustrate the will of the people.

King: I had understood there was to be a negotiation about the nature of the new government's policies.

Max: Yes, yes. That's what they said. Let's all be friends, they said, let's sit down and agree some policies. But when I told them what policies they had to agree, all hell broke loose.

King: Oh dear.

Max: You've never seen such a fuss outside a hen house. Cluck cluck, can't do this, some expert in Sweden thinks it'll make the planet warmer. Cluck cluck, can't do that, it might offend our Muslim brothers and sisters.

King: Perhaps they felt the nation was not yet ready for some of your policies. Your proposals for control of the news media, for example…

Max: Do you want a patriotic media or not? If you do, you have to find patriots to own and control it.

King: But do they have to be American patriots? Your list of approved owners did rather lean towards the transatlantic.

Max: They're Americans with a real stake in Britain's success. You can't own great chunks of a country and not care about its success, can you?

King: I suppose you could argue that the poor have a greater stake in Britain's success. They are rather stuck here. The wealthy can go somewhere else.

Max: How much of Britain do the poor own?

King: Very little, I believe.

Max: My case rests.

King: Yes. Well. You want a dissolution of Parliament, I take it?

Max: If it's not too much trouble.

King: If my Prime Minister advises it, then according to our unwritten constitution, I must accept that advice.

(MAX *makes to go*.)

Max: Good. It's been a pleasure.

King: Prime Minister…

Max: What?

King: I couldn't help noticing that electoral hostilities have already broken out. You appear to have referred to the previous Prime Minister as, and I quote, "the wretched Pam Jones and her clique of foreign moneylenders and gay lobbyists" and you called her a militant lesbian. I understand the veracity of this statement, to put it mildly, questionable.

Max: Your point being?

King:	Is she, in fact, a militant lesbian?
Max:	Quite possibly.
King:	Despite her husband being of the male persuasion?
Max:	May I ask what is the point of this interrogation?
King:	I wondered whether I might prevail upon you to moderate your speeches a little. When you say these things, people seem to take so much pleasure in repeating them.
Max:	A little *joie de vivre* on the part of the lumpen proletariat, very much *comme il faut*. Surely the king doesn't want to take the pleasures of the British worker away from him?
King:	No. No, not at all. My apologies. The robustness of political discourse is clearly beyond my remit. Well, Prime Minister, I shall see you after the election. To ask you to form another government, or, alternatively, not, as the case may be. Perhaps you might care to bring Mrs Moore with you next time?
Max:	I told you before, Mrs M never goes out. A real homebody, Mrs M, God bless her.
King:	There is a natural curiosity among the public about the wife of the Prime Minister. A curiosity which, I must admit, I share.
Max:	Have you been listening to rumours?
King:	No. No indeed. I make it a rule…
Max:	Good. It's bad enough having the reptiles from the media creeping around Mrs M, ooh, I wonder what she likes like, ooh, I wonder if she's pretty, I wonder if she's, you know, one of them. She doesn't want them around her. She's a home loving soul, and that's all anyone need know about her.
King:	Quite. Nothing could be more natural.
Max:	Good. I'd better be off if you don't mind. Few things to be getting on with.

King: Goodbye, Prime Minister.

Max: Bye.

 (MAX *Moore starts to leave.*)

King: Prime Minister.

Max: Sir?

King: These constitutional niceties. They may be antiquated, but we have no written constitution, and I sometimes feel the niceties are all that stands between us and...

Max: And what?

King: I don't know.

SCENE 2

SAMANTHA seated on a sofa or armchair. Enter MAX with two glasses of whisky, one of which he gives her before he sits.

Samantha: The Macallan Sherry Oak 18 year old, I hope?

Max: Five hundred quid a bottle, so it knows it's got to be good. Nothing's too good for my best adviser. How was my speech last night?

Samantha: Brilliant, Maxi. Just brilliant. Ready for the interview this afternoon?

Max: I certainly am. Tell me about it.

Samantha: It's for GB News. It's the only broadcast interview we do all campaign.

Max: The BBC can go cap in hand to our chums at GB News and beg for clips. I love it.

Samantha: Not just the BBC. We don't let any of the anti-British media near you. They'll be like "Max, just a minute", "Max, a quick word for Sky News," and they'll all be begging you to debate Pam Jones on television, and you smile and move on.

Max: Who's interviewing me?

Samantha: I am. People still think of me as a journalist. Of course some people will say I'm a bit too close to you to be credible.

Max: It's only the liberal elite does that sort of thinking. Our people don't give a toss.

Samantha: Exactly.

Max: I want to do it live.

Samantha: No. It's a pre-record.

Max: I'm much better live. Gets the adrenalin going. I did that speech last night live.

Samantha: I don't mind you doing a straightforward piece to camera live, but not an interview.

Max: I'm authentic. Pam Jones has to ask half a dozen committees before she blows her nose. With me, what you see is what you get. Pre-record, you lose the authenticity.

Samantha: In an interview, you need a safety net.

Max: I don't make mistakes. If I do, they're inspired mistakes. I know what the people want.

Samantha: I don't care about the people. Who raises money in the City for you?

Max: You, mostly.

Samantha: So listen to me. One mistake and you could throw away hundreds of millions of pounds.

Max: Still gives me a thrill.

Samantha: I know, Max. I know.

Max: Knowing they're out there as you speak, men envying you, women mooning over you, hanging on every word. You don't get that thrill with a pre-record.

Samantha: Live broadcasting, Max. There's nothing like it.

Max: There's only one thing better in the world. Doing it like the old days. Thousands of them in a bloody great hall, all of them stamping, shouting your name, and just you alone, under a spotlight, leading them, inspiring them, like a fucking God.

Samantha: We can get you one of those. But not today.

(But MAX is consumed by his own dream. He is delivering his speech to an invisible cheering crowd, in a thundering voice.)

Max: The English are sick of travelling second class. They're sick of apologising for being the greatest nation on earth. They're sick of being discriminated against in their own land. They want the place in the world that is their birthright.

Samantha: They want another glass of Macallan.

(The spell is broken. They look at each other and smile. He takes her empty glass and makes to go and refill it.)

Samantha: But there isn't time. We have to go.

Max: Quick one in the back of the car on the way to the studio?

Samantha: I think we've have had enough Macallan.

Max: I didn't mean the Macallan.

Samantha: I know.

(They look at each other for a moment then walk out arm in arm.)

SCENE 3

PAM Jones at her desk at home. Her desk lamp provides all the light there is. She is looking at her laptop, wearing earphones. We cannot see the screen as it is facing her and away from the audience. She is very tired. She speaks directly to the screen.

Pam: Thank you all for joining the meeting at such short notice. We've just had an unexpected second election thrown at us, and we've got to hit the ground running. We need a hard-hitting statement, and we need it fast.

You've got my draft in front of you. It's already had the benefit of amendments from most members of the shadow cabinet, from our business group and our trade union group, from all of the members of the national executive, from the Equality Group and all its constituent groups.

I need you to agree it now, without any more delay. Every minute counts. Every minute that Max Moore can dominate the news with no answer from us. Yes, Magdela? Oh, yes, I'm sorry, I forgot. First we must establish each other's preferred pronouns.

(*She mutters as she takes notes.*)

She/her. He/him. She/her. They. Thank you. Now about the text. Yes, Magdala? Yes. Only you see, Max Moore did say I was a militant lesbian, and it's a lie, and we do need to nail it… Yes, naturally there's nothing wrong with being a militant lesbian, it just happens that in my own case… Yes indeed, as you say, we need to be careful not to give the impression that our concern for equality is insufficiently gendered –

(*Stage lights gradually come on, and MICHAEL comes in quietly. He is wearing a dressing gown, and has come from his bed. PAM looks at him, smiles, and makes a gesture of despair.*)

Michael: Why are you still up? You're exhausted.

(PAM *looks at him and puts her finger to her lips.*)

Pam: (*To screen.*) Yes, Daniel? Daniel, it would take weeks to set up a subcommittee to examine our economic agenda in detail!

Michael: You haven't got a statement out yet? Heavens!

Pam: Yes, I know it's important not to make un-costed promises, but we have to promise something. Yes, the shadow chancellor trimmed them back to what he thought was responsible. Well, yes, you're right, if we say that, the *Daily Mail* will write that we're going to bankrupt the nation.

Michael: They're going to write that anyway, whatever you say.

Pam: They'll write that anyway, whatever we say. Fred, you wanted to say something? Yes, Fred, I think a trade union perspective on economic affairs would be very valuable. Can I suggest the rest of us turn off our videos while you give it to us? And mute ourselves, of course. That way we'll only have Fred on our screens and we can concentrate on the important points he has to make. Take your time, Fred.

(PAM *presses a key on her computer. Then she leans back, throws her arms out wide, and screams.*)

Michael: Have you been doing this all day?

Pam: Yep.

Michael: (*Imitating politicians.*) Ooooh, that's a bit too clear, can't we make it a bit obscure. Is your friend Magdala there?

Pam: Unfortunately, yes. There are several passages which she feels need further thought. She hasn't provided alternatives. She just thinks they need further thought. So I offer alternatives, and she says we're not quite there yet. It's very tiring.

Michael: I remember her visiting you when you were in hospital last year...

Pam: Hallo Pam, the national executive has instructed me to wish you a speedy recovery.

(They are both laughing by now in anticipation of the punchline.)

Michael: The motion was carried by 12 votes to nine with three abstentions.

Pam: Hang on, hang on.

(She has seen something on the screen and presses a button.)

Pam: That's very interesting, Fred, I wonder if you could expand on your point about equality at work. Thank you, the rest of us mute again please.

(She presses a button.)

Michael: Do you think some of them secretly want Max Moore to win the election?

Pam: Noooooo – but a lot of them can see a silver lining if he does. Who knows who might get my job?

Michael: Don't you wish you'd stayed in the classroom with me?

Pam: Do I wish I was still a teacher! Do I want to stop hitting myself on the head with a blunt instrument! Yes, I do, most of the time. But not all the time. Sometimes I remember that this is what I always wanted to do.

Michael: This is what you were made to do. Lots of people can make good teachers.

Pam: Not many as good as you, Michael. I knew I'd never be as good with children as you.

Michael: If you like children, it's the best job in the world. If you don't like children, it must be a horrible job.

Pam: People like you matter more in the end than people like me. If we get more head teachers like you, then the Max Moores won't get a chance with the next generation.

Michael: That's why you and I split the task of changing the world. Remember?

Pam: You'd become a head teacher and I'd become Prime Minister.

Michael: And we're half way there already.

(*They both laugh. They've made that joke before.*)

Michael: Seriously. Lots of people can make good teachers. Not many people can plot, and dissemble when they have to, and inspire when they have to, and never forget what they want to achieve in the end. You can do that.

Pam: Hang on.

(*She has seen something on the screen again and presses a button.*)

Pam: That's a really important point, Fred, and we'll take it on board. Did you give some thought to industrial democracy? I thought you might have done. Yes, please go ahead. Can we all mute ourselves and turn our cameras off please? Fred, you have the floor.

(*She switches off again.*)

Michael: Newspapers say we're going down.

Pam: Yes.

Michael: What are you going to do?

Pam: What I know how to do. Get all the factions behind me, which means getting an anodyne statement out tonight that won't alienate any of them, and then try and wake everyone up to the harm Max Moore will do if he gets an overall majority. And work and work and work, and hope it's enough.

Michael: It won't be.

Pam: It has to be. It matters too much for it not to be enough.

Michael: You know why it won't work?

Pam: (*Patiently.*) Tell me.

Michael: All right, I'm not a Westminster strategist, I think social
             media was invented by Satan and polls are things
             they hang telephone wires on. But I know something,
             and it's this. You won't save the country from Max
             Moore by hoping people will realise that at least
             you're not as bad as he is. You won't do it by being
             statesmanlike and cautious, especially when you've
             just spent four months in government doing just that
             and achieving bugger all.

Pam: Not much you can do when there's no money and you
             have to keep a coalition together...

Michael: Promise that they'll get richer, the filthy rich will get
             poorer. You can deliver that. Remember what your
             speeches were like before you became leader? The
             way you had of inspiring people, giving them real
             hope, showing them just how dreadful the alternative
             was. Before you got all those experts round you and
             they said, enough of the fireworks, it's time to be
             statesmanlike, time to show you're the grownup in the
             room.

Pam: I can't go back...

Michael: Why not?

Pam: Years of building the anti-Moore coalition, persuading
             everyone to come on board, I could throw all that
             away with one speech.

Michael: The one speech that might do the job.

SCENE 4

Britons First logo appears on a screen. SAMANTHA brings in a coffee table, and sets a pint of beer on one side, and a glass of white wine on the other. She sits in front of the wine, and MAX comes in and sits in front of the pint.

Samantha   If there's a problem, I'll stop you, you say the sentence again without the dodgy bit, and I can edit later. Camera's over there, see it? Look directly at it during some of the heartfelt bits for a soundbite, otherwise look at me. Say "Britons First" a lot. Ok?

(*He turns to where she said the camera was, and gives a ghastly smile.*)

Max: God, I could do it so much better live.

Samantha: Ready? Off we go. Max Moore, thank you for giving us your time today.

Max: You're very welcome. Always a pleasure to talk to a distinguished journalist like you. What are you doing after the show, Samantha, if you've got a minute I could give you one in the green room?

(*She looks at him reproachfully. He smiles his naughty-boy smile.*)

Max: I got the safety net, I might as well use it. All right, cue me in again, I'll be a good boy.

Samantha: Max Moore, thank you for giving us your time today.

Max: Always a pleasure to talk to you, Samantha.

Samantha: I want to ask you about your slogan "Britons First." What exactly do you mean by it?

Max: "Britons First" means exactly what it says, Samantha. "Britons First." We're tired of giving the best of everything to foreigners. We're tired of bowing down to the sweepings of the streets of Damascus and Delhi and Dakar, and saying, please Mr Foreigner, trample all over us. We're tired of raising foreigners to the top of the tree. Do you know how many so-called

British organisations have Jewish and Muslim
leadership…

Samantha: Cosmopolitan leadership.

Max: Do you know how many so-called British
organisations have cosmopolitan leadership?

Samantha: How many?

Max: For heaven's sake.

Samantha: I thought you had a figure.

Max: Of course I haven't got a bloody figure.

Samantha: All right, take it from "do you know how many."

Max: Do you know how many so-called British
organisations have cosmopolitan leadership? It would
horrify you. As for the so-called intellectuals who think
they know better than you and me. I'm done with
being lectured by… how do I say "a gang of lefty
Jews?"

Samantha: The North London metropolitan elite.

Max: I'm done with being lectured by the North London
metropolitan elite.

Samantha: There's been criticism of your plan to hire American
companies to run Britain's civil service.

Max: What I want to do, Samantha, is to get the very best
Anglo Saxon business brains in the world to get Great
Britain PLC back on top of the world, and Put Britons
First. It's time to stop discriminating against the wealth
creators and the billionaires. When did it become
fashionable to be poor, I wonder?

Samantha: Thank you, that's very clear. Now, your opponents
say you don't care about discrimination.

Max: People who say that don't know me. I've faced
discrimination. I've always been an outsider, and I
always will be. When I left school and went into the
City to make a bob or two, I was horrified to find that
the City is stiff with men who went to school at Eton.

They said to me, where were you at school? And I had to say: Highgate.

Samantha: You suffered for not being an old Etonian?

Max: The Etonians talked their own language, hung out with their own, promoted their own. There is dreadful discrimination against the minor public schools. I got overlooked for jobs, for perks, for promotion. And I'm not going to lie, it hurt. But I fought it, and it made me stronger.

Samantha: And we all admire you for it.

Max: I had to do it all again, years later, when I went into Parliament and they said, "Where did you go to school?" and I told them, and all the lefties sneered at me because it wasn't Grunge Street sink school, where most of them went. But I fought the good fight, and now I want to fight it for you. For all of you.

Samantha: Put a bit more into the last bit. Look at the camera.

Max: But I fought the good fight, and now I want to fight it for you. For all of you.

Samantha: You want a country where everyone is equal.

Max: A country where Christians feel comfortable. A country where white men no longer feel discriminated against.

Samantha: Is it ok to ask the Jack Bulldog question?

Max: Yes, I've got a line.

Samantha: Max Moore, are you willing to co-operate with people like Jack Bulldog and his White Knights of St George, who set fire to mosques and encourage their young men to carry weapons?

Max: I want to be really clear about this. Jack Bulldog is a scamp. No two ways about it. Of course he's a patriot, he comes from good English working class stock. But he's got it wrong. Badly wrong.

Samantha: So he'll never be allowed into Britons First?

Max: We'll give that question a miss, if you don't mind.

Samantha: Sorry.

Max: I don't want any trace of that question…

Samantha: Don't worry. Your enemies say you don't respect women.

Max: Heavens, no. Cheer the place up no end, a few pretty girls.

Samantha: (*Wearily.*) Start again.

Max: What would men be without women? They'd be scarce, that's what they'd be. You sure about after the show?

Samantha: We haven't got all day.

Max: Sorry. Give me the cue again.

Samantha: Is it true that you don't respect women?

Max: No, it absolutely is not. Just because I won't mouth all the proper phrases the liberal elite tell us we've got to say… I'll tell you this much though. If it's a crime to fancy women, if it's a crime to want them, to love and cherish them, if it's a crime to lust after them, fetch the chains now (*He holds his hands in front of him as though bound.*) and haul me off to the dungeons, because I break the law every day, every hour. But that doesn't mean I don't respect them. (*Turns to look at camera.*) I respect women. Deeply. (*Pause.*) That ok?

Samantha: Can we talk about Mrs M?

Max: Do we have to?

Samantha: We have to say something, Max.

Max: I respect women. Deeply. If I didn't, my wonderful wife would have left me years ago. She's made the choice to be very private, to bring up our two young sons secretly, not to have her name plastered all over the papers, and I respect that choice.

Samantha: Is that all we can do?

Max: It's the bloody limit, bloody reptiles prying into my private life.

Samantha: All right, we'll leave it. Will you bring women into your government at the top level?

Max: You'll be the first, Samantha, you know that...

Samantha: I do, but I'm supposed to be an independent political journalist here, it won't sound good. Let's start again. Will you bring women into your government at the top level?

Max: I certainly will.

Samantha: But not, I suppose, the most prominent woman in politics, the Leader of the Opposition, Pam Jones.

Max: They call her the Leader of the Opposition, and that's what she is, the Leader of the Opposition to Britain. And as for her private life, I could tell you a few things...

Samantha: No, you couldn't.

Max: Why on earth not? It's true.

Samantha: Is it?

Max: She can't prove it's not.

Samantha: If you want to shame a woman about sex, you don't do it yourself, you get a woman to do it. They taught me that at the *Daily Mail*.

Max: Can't I...

Samantha: No. Come on, concentrate, next question coming up. Tell me about the real Max Moore. Where he came from, what made him what he is today.

Max: I come from a very ordinary background. Home counties, father a stockbroker, off to board at prep school when I was seven, just like everyone else. It was tough, but it was the making of me.

Samantha: Tough in what way?

(As the next section of dialogue progresses, MAX

seems to forget the camera. He is bringing up his demons.)

Max: My father knew what he was doing. Took me out of the nursery, out of the arms of my mother and my nanny, put me on a hard bed in a dormitory full of other boys, some of them crying all night for their mothers. Toughen me up, you see. Cruel to be kind. In my first week the other boys started calling me "Cissie" and the name stuck. For the next six years I'd hear it from matins to vespers. Hissing, tormenting. "Cissie, Cissie." Of course, I did what any self-respecting English schoolboy would do, I put up my fists, and one day one of them broke my nose, it's still a bit bent. I remember the boy who did that, I know where he works now... You can't use this stuff.

Samantha: You bet we can't. Aren't you glad I didn't let you do it live? Let's get back on track. You've said that your public school was what prepared you for government. What do you mean?

Max: That time at my prep school taught me something important, and it was this. There will always be a victim, and the trick in life is to make sure it's not you. So I got to my public school, and looked around and there was a spotty little boy no one liked, and I made sure he was the victim. Then I found the toughest boy in my year, and made him my best friend. That taught me the best lesson in statecraft any Prime Minister could have. Which is the biggest and toughest and richest country? The USA. We're going to cling to the USA and make them our best friend and hug them close. With me as Prime Minister, Britain will never be that spotty little boy everyone picks on.

Samantha: I think we're done. Let's do the closing shot.

Max: Britons First.

Samantha: Let's drink to that.

> (*They raise their glasses to toast each other and look directly at the camera.*)

Max and Samantha: Britons first.

> (*They look at the camera and hold the pose for a few seconds.*)

SCENE 5

SAMANTHA's flat. MAX and SAMANTHA enter, a little unsteadily. They have been at what we guess was a good party. MAX is notably more dishevelled than when we last saw him, and his tie is now hanging out of his pocket. MAX is singing, SAMANTHA joins in after a couple of lines.

Max and Samantha:
>Rugby may be more clever,
>Harrow may make more row,
>But we'll row for ever,
>Steady from stroke to bow,
>And nothing in life shall sever,
>The chain that is round us now,
>And nothing in life shall sever,
>The chain that is round us now.

Max: Consider our campaign well and truly launched.

Samantha: Did anyone notice we left the party together?

Max: Do we care?

Samantha: Probably not. It would destroy any other politician, but it doesn't seem to do you any harm.

Max: Trust Henry and Geraldine to lay on a good spread. Château Mouton Rothschild 2006, no less. Between £400 and £500 a bottle, I'd say. You know Geraldine and I used to...

Samantha: Before she married Henry?

Max: Well... There may have been the teeniest bit of overlap. Know what I mean?

Samantha: Is there a woman under 40 in London you haven't had sex with?

Max: Quite possibly. Give me time. Shall we round off the evening with a drop of the Macallan?

Samantha: Not yet.

Max: Oh dear. You want to talk business. All right, what is it?

Samantha: There was another call from Mrs M this morning.

Max: Oh God.

Samantha: I didn't want to tell you before the interview.

Max: What does she want now? It's costing me a fortune, sending the two boys to Eton. Masters of the universe, her sons are going to be.

Samantha: Apparently last term's fees weren't paid.

Max: I thought we had that covered. Some guy in Silicon Valley.

Samantha: Apparently someone told him what Eton was.

Max: Who would do a thing like that?

Samantha: He was furious. You'll have to cover a couple of terms yourself.

Max: I've got a liquidity problem.

Samantha: You always have a liquidity problem.

Max: You're the fundraiser. Isn't there a hedge fund you can tap up?

Samantha: It may have escaped your notice, but there's an election on. We need every penny we can raise.

Max: All right, I'll find the money. Is that all?

Samantha: It's all she actually asked for but I think she's beginning to realise just how much trouble she could cause us. It might help if you spoke to her.

Max: In what way might it help for me to be ear-bashed for half an hour about what a shit I am? She can't do anything, she doesn't know who to talk to.

Samantha: She doesn't have to know. News organisations have whole teams looking for her.

Max: Where are they looking?

Samantha: Favourite right now seems to be Glastonbury.

Max: Glastonbury's a nice town. Lots of things to see in Glastonbury. You could gently nudge that on along a bit if you like.

Samantha: I'm doing that. But it won't keep us safe forever.

Max: It just needs to keep us safe til polling day. After that I control the news.

Samantha: We have to keep the lid on til then. Which is tricky. She seems to be in love with you.

Max: Are you in love with me?

Samantha: Not in the slightest.

Max: Half the women in Britain are though.

Samantha: Will that do?

Max: That'll do.

SCENE 6

A desk in the middle of the stage with the back of what we discover to be an auto cue on it. Screen at back says "Vote Progressive Alliance." Enter PAM. She is wearing earphones. She looks into the auditorium, searching for the camera.

Pam: It's a pre-record but you want to do it as live? We do it in one take as though it were live? Ok, I can do that. That's the autocue?

(She points to the desk.)

Pam: Won't it be a bit static, me sitting behind the desk? Yes, I see. I suppose you're right, that's a good look. Steady, trustworthy.

(She sits at the desk, takes off the earphones and puts them out of sight under the desk.)

Pam: Ready when you are. Good evening. You, as voters, have a really important decision to take in the next few days. I hope you will cast your vote for the Progressive Alliance because… Oh, for heaven's sake. This stuff's no good. Start again. I'm going off piste.

(She gets up and walks round to the front of the desk.)

Pam: In this election you're choosing freedom or slavery. If you elect Max Moore, you're choosing slavery. Here's how he will take away your freedoms.

First, Max Moore wants us to hate each other, because a divided population is easier to control. That way, he hopes, we'll forget what really divides us. It's not that we're black or white, men or women. It's not what we like to do in bed, or who we like to do it with.

What divides us is money. The richest 1% of Britons own a quarter of the country's wealth. The poorest 20% own just half a per cent. Max Moore is for the 1%. We're for the rest.

Moore says the 1% are wealth creators. But the ultra-rich don't create wealth. They shuffle it around, mostly to themselves.

Second, Max Moore lies all the time. You know that, and he knows you know it. So why does he bother? I'll tell you. He's going to lie and lie until no one knows what the truth looks like anymore. People who don't know what's true and what's a lie can be made to do anything Max wants.

Third, he wants to steal the state, and hand it over to whoever bankrolls him. He wants everything this country's got, to give to his wealthy backers. You'll end up paying for your children's school, the doctor when you need treatment, the police to come round when you're mugged, the fire brigade when your house catches fire. And it won't matter that you've already paid for it with your taxes, because Max Moore is going to take it all away.

He says, shrink the state, leave it only capable of making war and incapable of making welfare. But he doesn't really want to shrink the state. He wants to steal it. And when Max Moore owns the army and the police, who will protect you when Max Moore turns on you?

There's a better way. We'll take money away from Max Moore's rich friends, and give it to people like you. The state will own more, not less, and it'll be controlled by people you elect. Government can make your lives better. But only if you elect people who want to make your lives better.

Britain's awash with money. We can use it to help our people. Or we can hand it over to Max Moore and his friends. Which do you want?

Thank you, and good night.

(*Lights go off and she starts to walk slowly towards the exit.*)

Pam: Michael, what have you made me do? (*But she does not sound too unhappy about it.*)

SCENE 7

The KING at his desk. Enter MAX. KING stands.

King: Prime Minister.

Max: Sir.

(*He sits.* KING *coughs.* MAX *remembers and stands up again.*)

King: Please sit down, Prime Minister.

Max: Thank you, sir.

(*They both sit.*)

King: Our association, as monarch and Prime Minister, has been short. I would like to take this opportunity to wish you and Mrs Moore a happy retirement. Perhaps we may meet again, under happier circumstances.

Max: What on earth are you talking about?

King: I take it you are here to resign as Prime Minister, and to advise me to send for Ms Jones.

Max: Why would I do that?

King: The normal practice, when the Prime Minister loses a general election, is for him to come to the monarch and advise him to send for the leader of the biggest party in Parliament.

Max: Who says I lost the election?

King: I am advised by my constitutional expert Lord Thistlethwaite that the loss of a parliamentary majority, and the election of more Members of Parliament from another Party than were elected from your own Party, is considered to constitute losing the election. It's a theory that does have a certain attractive logic to it.

Max: Who says they got more MPs than me?

King: I heard it on the ten o'clock news.

Max: On the BBC, I suppose?

King:	It would appear to be the general consensus among the news media.
Max:	It's pretty narrow though, isn't it?
King:	Yes indeed. Right up to the last few seats, it seemed it could go either way. I am informed that an unexpectedly forthright last minute broadcast from Ms Jones may have been the deciding factor.
Max:	Did you hear that broadcast?
King:	No. I followed my Prime Minister's advice, and avoided exposure to Ms Jones's broadcasts.
Max:	It was full of horrible, hateful personal attacks. That sort of thing debases our politics.
King:	Yes. Well, I believe some of our political discourse may be more vigorous than one might have wished, but I have always been advised to make no comment on such matters.
Max:	As King, you should condemn it.
King:	Had you not advised me to refrain from watching her broadcasts, I might be in a better position to do so.
Max:	You don't need to hear them. I'm informing you, as your first minister, that they crossed a line.
King:	Are you still my first minister?
Max:	I am.
King:	I mention the matter because, you see, precedent would indicate that this meeting signals an end to your tenure.
Max:	Your majesty. Sir. Tell me this. Are you a constitutional monarch?
King:	Yes. Yes indeed. Very much so. Absolutely.
Max:	As a constitutional monarch, are you under an obligation to take the advice of your first minister?
King:	Indeed I am.
Max:	Therefore, when I tell you that I am still your first

minister, your constitutional duty is to accept my advice in this matter. To do otherwise would be flying in the face of democracy.

King: Surely we must face the awkward fact that Ms Jones won the election.

Max: It may look to you as though Pam Jones won the election.

King: I understood she has an overall majority of seventeen.

Max: Yes, but there were irregularities in the voting in several constituencies.

King: How many constituencies?

Max: Eighteen.

King: Eighteen?

Max: Eighteen.

King: That's very...

Max: Very what?

King: Awkward.

Max: Naturally, I can't desert my post with this dreadful stain on our democratic process unresolved. I have to oversee the investigation into these irregularities.

King: I see.

Max: Thank you for being so understanding. Now, if you'll excuse me, I have a lot to do. It's no picnic, being your first minister, I can tell you that for nothing.

(MAX *gets up to leave.*)

King: Prime Minister.

Max: Yes?

King: (*Clearly uncomfortable.*) It's these constitutional niceties.

Max: Exactly what constitutional niceties are we referring to here?

King:	I have at the moment no evidence before me of any electoral malpractice.
Max:	I'm your first minister and I'm informing you that there has been serious electoral malpractice.
King:	Nonetheless…
Max:	I hope you're not suggesting I'm lying to you?
King:	No. No, no, no. No such thing shall be suggested. However, could it be that, in an excess of zeal, you have inadvertently overstepped the bounds of constitutional propriety. Is that possible?
Max:	No.
King:	Prime Minister. Lord Thistlethwaite is good enough to draw up scenarios for me so that I may be equipped to deal with them.
Max:	Very interesting, and another time I'd love to have a bit of chinwag about it, but right now I have a few things I need to get on with.
King:	One of these scenarios is precisely the situation in which we now find ourselves, in which the Prime Minister, having lost the election – or at least, to all appearances having lost it – then seeks to retain his post while balloting irregularities are considered. Lord Thistlethwaite advised me that such a course, were it to be proposed, would be at variance with our unwritten constitution.
Max:	Did he also point out that it was your duty, as a constitutional monarch, to follow the advice given by your Prime Minister?
King:	He did. My constitutional duty is to accept your advice to send for Ms Jones. But this, naturally, depends upon you giving me such advice. As I understand it, you decline so to advise me. This places me on the horns of a dilemma.
Max:	There's no dilemma at all. If you act against the advice of your elected Prime Minister, you're spitting

in the face of democracy.

King: But surely...

Max: Remember what happened to the first King Charles when he wouldn't do what Parliament wanted?

King: Prime Minister...

Max: I'm not serious. No one's going to cut your head off.

King: I'm delighted to hear it.

Max: You're going to be fine, so long as you do your duty, which is to do whatever I tell you. Now, if you'll excuse me...

King: Prime Minister...

Max: Yes?

King: There is one more matter.

Max: Yes?

King: It is a matter of some delicacy.

Max: Yes?

King: It concerns, in short, the matter of your, well...

Max: Yes?

King: Lord Thistlethwaite considers it advisable that I should raise with you the matter of your personal conduct.

Max: Does he indeed?

King: Indeed he does. Prime Minister, it would appear that your marital arrangements are less conventional than those of most of your predecessors.

Max: Unlike yours, of course, which no one could ever have criticised.

King: That is hardly the point.

Max: You're referring, I suppose to the recent report by a journalist who claims to have found Mrs M living in a suburb of Bangkok. An entirely unsubstantiated claim.

King: And in fact, false?

Max:	I said it was unsubstantiated.
King:	But not untrue?
Max:	Mrs M suffers from bronchitis. Her doctors advised that the air in Thailand would do her good.
King:	Then the claim that she is in fact Thai by birth is false?
Max:	I hope you don't hold her ethnicity against her.
King:	No, no…
Max:	I would not want to think that the King was racist.
King:	Absolutely not. Quite the reverse. It would be most shocking were I to be racially discriminatory in any shape or form whatsoever.
Max:	Good. Then I take it we may consider the matter closed.
King:	I hesitate to mention the other aspect or the reports.
Max:	Hesitate to your heart's content.
King:	Yet I feel…
Max:	Hesitating is good. Shutting up is even better.
King:	I feel I must mention the matter of her age.
Max:	And what the hell has that got to do with you?
King:	Well, were there to be – I speak hypothetically, you understand – were there to be some question of criminal proceedings against you, then it would be Lord Thistlethwaite's opinion…
Max:	What do you mean, criminal proceedings?
King:	Prime Minister, the claim has been made that, according to her birth certificate, she was just fifteen years old when you and she were blessed with your first child.
Max:	Birth certificates can be forged.
King:	Indeed they can. So may I take it that in this case…
Max:	Pin back your ears, Charlie boy, because you don't

want to miss a syllable of what I'm about to tell you. You've got a pretty good life here. You live in the lap of luxury, waited on hand and foot, doing bugger all except waving and smiling and trying not to make too big a tit of yourself, and we let you get away with it because, let's face it, you're useful. All the proles in god-forsaken holes like Salford, or Stoke on Trent, or Sunderland, think you're wonderful because you're the king, and we can wheel you out every so often to sprinkle a bit of stardust on whatever we want to do. But we could turn on you. Those crowds I had to come through to get into this nice comfortable palace of yours, they were shouting for Max Moore. They weren't shouting for king fucking Charles the fucking third, they were shouting for me. You cross Max Moore, they'll tear you to pieces. Do you understand me?

(*Suddenly we hear God Save the King sung loudly.*)

King: Where does that come from?

(MAX *picks up his phone and the singing stops abruptly mid-sentence, or, better, mid-word. We realise it is* MAX's *ringtone.*)

Max: Hallo. Yes. How much damage? Ok. There in ten.

(*He puts the phone away.*)

Max: They've burned down the Houses of Parliament.

King: They've... Who? Who has burned down the Houses of Parliament?

Max: The Muslims, of course.

King: Are you sure?

Max: You can see the smoke from that window. How much more evidence do you want?

King: Yes, but...

Max: I'm going over there. People expect the PM to be on the spot in a crisis like this.

King: I'll come with you. People expect the monarch...

Max: You don't move from Buckingham Palace, do you understand me? You don't talk to anyone. You tell your press office you're awaiting a full report from me. You sit here and you stay shtum.

King: Prime Minister...

Max: There's a demonstration against the burning of the Houses of Parliament starting up right now.

King: How could that be organised so quickly?

Max: And if they see you, God knows what they might do.

(*He goes out. KING gets out his phone.*)

King: Could you ask Lord Thistlethwaite to come and see me? Please tell him it's a matter of some urgency.

SCENE 8

SAMANTHA pushes onstage a pub bar, with a couple of hand pumps on it. Behind it, a big poster says "We Serve BRITONS FIRST". The last two words are in big type.

Samantha: (*Speaking to the camera.*) Ok? A bit to the left?

    (*She pushes it a bit to the left and looks up at the camera. Apparently the camera operator is satisfied, because* SAMANTHA *gives a thumbs up sign. She places a small pub table and a chair at the front of the stage and goes behind the bar. Enter* MAX.)

Max: Pint of best please, my love.

    (*She pretends to pour the beer, and hands him a full pint glass.*)

Max: What's the damage?

Samantha: No charge for you, Max. You're all this country's got right now.

Max: Well, that's very British of you, I must say. Very British indeed.

    (*As he speaks to the camera, he carries his beer forward and sits at the table.*)

Max: You don't mind my addressing you from my local, do you? It's where I feel at home. That great Englishman G.K. Chesterton put it well:

> St George he was for England,
> And before he killed the dragon
> He drank a pint of English ale
> Out of an English flagon.

It's the simple things that make life worthwhile. The things we take for granted. Like going out to the local for a pint at the end of a hard day. How much longer will we be able to do that, I wonder?

The liberal elite have their fingers on Britain's throat. They want to take everything away that puts the great into Great Britain. And yesterday they showed us who they really are. They attacked the Houses of Parliament – the sacred centuries-old symbol of British democracy.

But they've reckoned without one thing. They've reckoned without the pride and the fighting spirit that once made Britain feared and respected in every corner of the globe.

Today, I issued what I call a "shooting decree." It allows police to shoot on sight when they see enemies of the people going about their wicked business.

Why do we have to do something that I know some of you might regard as un-British? I'll tell you. If we don't, then every time the police go after the wreckers, gangs of liberal lawyers will all be waving their writs about, all saying, can't do that, officer, you're trampling on their sacred civil liberties.

I can't ask our brave police officers to go after the liberal mob if they have to worry about what might happen afterwards.

I know you understand. And I know too that the cream of our young men are listening to me now, and they are saying to themselves: how can I help? what can I do? Well, there is something you can do.

We are lucky to have in this country a small but committed paramilitary organisation called the White Knights of St George. Today I spoke to their leader, a man called Jack Bulldog, and I made him an emergency supernumerary commissioner of police. His men will work alongside the established police force. They will be provided with guns, and they will help keep the peace in our streets and in our beautiful countryside.

And Mr Bulldog's force needs more men. At the end of this broadcast you'll see a link on your screen. Follow that link, and apply to join up today. If you're accepted, you'll be helping to put the Great back into Great Britain.

Cheers.

(*He takes a gulp of his beer.*)

Samantha: Another one, Max? On the house.

Max: Don't mind if I do.

(*She hands him another pint. They pause for a moment with the pint between them, grinning at the camera. Then they break the pose.*)

Max: Will that do?

Samantha: That'll do.

(*She pushes the bar offstage.*)

SCENE 9

Prison. Sounds of clanging doors, on screen a visual of prison bars. A bench. On it sit PAM Jones and KING Charles, facing the audience.

Pam: Is your cell comfortable, your majesty?

King: Under the circumstances I don't think the formality of calling me "your majesty" is entirely necessary.

Pam: Charles…

King: Sir will be quite adequate. I'm not sure what the general standard of prison accommodation is, but it seems to me to be quite unnecessarily uncomfortable. However, at least I have it to myself. Most of the other inmates in my vicinity appear to have to share their cells. Do you know why they've brought us here?

Pam: No idea. But it's better than sitting in my cell, wondering what's going to happen next.

King: Ms Jones, may I ask you… I overheard a discussion… the appalling notion was suggested that physical pressure might be applied to you in order to render you amenable to… I hope you understand that I would consider it an outrage…

Pam: They brought to my cell the heavily muscled people whose skill it is to persuade one to divulge information. I asked what information they wanted, and I gave it to them, in full and with copious corroborating detail. I added that whatever they wanted me to sign, I would sign. But everyone would know why I had signed it. So they left. Since then, beating has not been mentioned, except by my cellmate, who is large and unpredictable and once terrorised most of Brixton, I understand. I think I have won her round with a few kindnesses.

King: That it should come to this! But Ms Jones, this nightmare may be nearing its end. The Chief Justice of the Supreme Court has made clear her robust condemnation of your incarceration.

Pam: Ah, that would explain it.

King: Explain what?

Pam: She's in the next cell to mine. I thought I heard her voice last night.

King: Oh.

(*Enter* SAMANTHA.)

Samantha: Good afternoon, Pam.

Pam: Samantha! What are you doing here?

Samantha: Aren't you going to introduce me to his majesty?

Pam: Samantha is Max Moore's favourite political journalist, sir.

Samantha: Your majesty. Is that the right thing to call you?

King: In the circumstances, your majesty is probably the appropriate form of address.

Pam: Why are you here, Samantha? I don't suppose you're writing a piece about how shocking it is that we should be locked up like criminals.

Samantha: That's exactly what I'm going to do, Pam.

Pam: You're not finally turning on Max, after all these years?

Samantha: I'm going to write about how wrong it is to keep the Leader of the Opposition locked up.

King: You might perhaps give the king a passing mention.

Samantha: Ah, well, that's a harder one.

King: Why?

Samantha: No one knows you're here.

King: Surely my press office must have said something about my absence?

Samantha: They have. Max told your press office you were seriously ill, but he also told them that the king's illness must be kept secret. So Max said they should invent a cover story. And they did. They're telling everyone you're staying in Buckingham Palace so as to be available when your country needs you.

Pam: So the press office is busy covering up what they think is the truth. And what they're actually covering up...

Samantha: ...is itself a cover-up. Delicious, isn't it?

King: Someone must have noticed I'm not around. Lord Thistlethwaite must have noticed my absence. You couldn't keep him quiet unless you put him...

(*He looks at* SAMANTHA's *impassive face and understands.*)

King: I see. But it's bound to leak. There are prison guards. There are other prisoners.

Samantha: That's why you get the luxury of a cell to yourself, and a man brings you all your meals in your cell. Always the same man, you'll have noticed. Pam's imprisonment, on the other hand, is front page news.

Pam: What are they saying?

Samantha: Electoral malpractice. Trying to steal a democratic election. Serious stuff. Your MPs don't like it, of course. They're trying to say you were framed. Well, quite a lot of them are.

Pam: Magdela has seen the main chance, I suppose.

Samantha: There's a group of them, and we're giving them some friendly help. They're briefing non-attributably that you kept the details of electoral organisation from them, and they always had their suspicions. With friends like that...

Pam: I don't need enemies like you.

Samantha: I'm not your enemy. I really have written that article. It's ready to go.

Pam: Show me.

(PAM *reaches for* SAMANTHA's *phone.* SAMANTHA *puts it behind her back.*)

Samantha: Uh oh. Nice try, but you know perfectly well you're not allowed access to a phone. I'll read you my intro. (*Reads.*) "Red Pam Jones, hard left leader of the Progressive Alliance, is languishing in jail. Now, I hold no brief for Red Pam. If she had succeeded in stealing the election, she'd bankrupt us all and hand us in chains to one of her pet foreign governments. But prison's not the right place for her. Max Moore should release her today – on strict conditions, of course."

Pam: Thank you.

Samantha: Ok, so it's not exactly how you'd want me to write it, but this is the way to get you out of here.

Pam: I see.

Samantha: Look. I'm here to help you.

Pam: Really?

Samantha: Let's start by accepting that Max is Prime Minister. You may not like that, but you can't change it.

King: He can't be Prime Minister. He hasn't got a parliamentary majority.

Samantha: He will have by tomorrow.

Pam: Don't tell me. Exactly eighteen of my MPs have been found to have been elected fraudulently.

Samantha: Nineteen in fact.

Pam: You only needed eighteen.

Samantha: Max likes to be sure. One of ours might drop dead.

Pam: I see.

Samantha: If you were to resign your seat in Parliament and give me the exclusive story about how you're giving up politics, I'd put that into this article. Then Max could gracefully bow to public opinion and let you out of prison. You could go back to teaching. You could teach at Michael's school. You'd like that. So would he.

Pam: How would I explain why I'm giving up politics?

Samantha: All this electoral fraud happened on your watch, didn't it? Isn't the appropriate response to resign?

Pam: There wasn't any fraud. You know that's the truth.

Samantha: Truth is kind of liquid right now.

Pam: What's to stop me making trouble outside?

Samantha: Did you know that Ofsted has been looking at Michael's school?

Pam: Oh, I see.

Samantha: Some of the parents have complained that the teaching there is unpatriotic. It could easily be the end of Michael's career. If only he'd told his history department to stick to the middle ages!

Pam: I see.

Samantha: Try to see it from where Max stands. The country's in crisis. The Houses of Parliament have been burned down.

Pam: Wonder who might have done that.

Samantha: Some suspects have already been detained.

Pam: I thought they might have been.

Samantha: In a crisis, the government needs to be able to act quickly.

Pam: Don't tell me. You need an enabling law.

Samantha: It's a temporary measure. It just means that the government can make laws swiftly and decisively, without having to wait for an act to trundle its weary way through the House of Commons and half a dozen committees and then through the House of Lords. And it means we can do things without the Supreme Court stepping in and saying, can't do that, it's contrary to ye olde Bread and Ale Act of 1266 or something. It's for a strictly defined period.

Pam: How long?

Samantha: Four years.

Pam: Four years? My God!

Samantha: Parliament is debating it now. Some of your MPs are being rather obstructive, but we'll get it through. We have the votes.

Pam: No committee stage, of course.

Samantha: We try to avoid too many bureaucratic obstacles. This is a new streamlined business-oriented way of governing.

Pam: And – let me guess – you get it through the House of Lords by threatening to give voting seats to hundreds of your people. And that's where his maj. here comes in. You need the king to agree to that.

Samantha: No. We won't need to trouble his majesty with that. Quite a lot of voting peers have found themselves unavoidably detained on the way to the house.

King: That is disgraceful. Deplorable. Unprecedented.

Samantha: However, we will then need to ask his majesty if he will graciously give the Act his royal assent.

King: I think, in the circumstances, this might place me in a very difficult position.

Samantha: Do you feel you ought to consult Lord Thistlethwaite?

King: I would certainly need to know Lord Thistlethwaite's view before pronouncing definitively.

Samantha: That's very right and proper. One of my colleagues has visited the noble lord to discuss the advice he might give you.

King: It's hardly proper for one of your colleagues to act as intermediary. I must be permitted to consult Lord Thistlethwaite personally.

Samantha: Of course you must. There is a gentleman outside who can guide you to another room where I believe the noble lord waits upon you.

King: Well, in that case – Ms Jones, perhaps you might excuse me.

Pam: Of course. Goodbye, sir.

Samantha: Goodbye, your majesty. That door there, please.

(*Exit* KING.)

Pam: (*Wearily.*) What have you got on Thistlethwaite?

Samantha: He has a son. A rather foolish young man with some unwise business connections.

Pam: What are you getting out of all this, Samantha?

Samantha: I'll be Chancellor of the Exchequer tomorrow.

Pam: You can't be Chancellor. You're not an MP.

Samantha: It's high time these outdated bureaucratic obstacles to progress were swept away.

Pam: You don't know the first thing about economics.

Samantha: We're getting rid of the tyranny of experts.

Pam: I don't think I realised just how cynical you are.

Samantha: You wouldn't want to be my enemy. And you don't have to be, Pam. We've had fun together, you and I. You showed me the best bar in Westminster.

Pam: The Woolsack.

Samantha: That crummy drinking den in the basement where two women from different parties can drink a bottle of wine each, laugh together, gossip, and stagger home afterwards with no one knowing what was said.

Pam: We had some good evenings.

Samantha: Pam, what Max had in mind for you was a lot worse than what I'm offering. I had to fight for this deal.

Pam: I believe you. I'm probably one of the few people who knows what you really think of Max.

Samantha: The only one. Honestly.

Pam: The middle aged bore in every pub, sitting over his gin and tonic and boasting pathetically – look, I got one over the greengrocer, I got a woman to go to bed with me.

Samantha: Thank God your party let us brand you as "woke." Now the most tedious saloon bar bore in Surrey can rebrand himself as "gloriously un-woke."

Pam: And you're willing to make someone like that Prime Minister?

Samantha: To you and me, Max is a vain, ignorant product of the English public school system, but there's a magic there that we can't see. Men look up to him. Boys model themselves on him. Women swoon over him. He's got something. If only we knew exactly what he's got, we'd bottle it, then we wouldn't need him any more.

Pam: Why do you need him anyway? He'd be nothing without the money you raise for him. If your City friends stopped funding him...

Samantha: We need lower taxes on business. We need to shrink the state, cut public spending, get rid of nine-tenths of the public sector, get rid of unproductive things like welfare payments and state schools, and put business and finance in the driving seat again. That's what we made Max for. Once he's delivered that, we'll ditch him and politics will be back to normal.

Pam: And when Max has delivered – you really think you'll be able to put the toothpaste back in the tube?

Samantha: Give him a couple of pretty girls to play with, he'll forget all about government.

Pam: You're playing with fire.

Samantha: Why don't you let us try, Pam? You can't stop us, so make it easy on yourself. Keep your head down.

Make your husband keep his down too. You're happy together, you and Michael. I know you are.

Pam: And let your lot trash our democracy.

Samantha: Do you really believe all that democracy stuff? The sacred principle of nose-counting? Everyone must have exactly the same vote, the rich and the poor, the Einsteins and the idiots? When you see the poor, the unemployed and the marginally employed, in little huddles on street corners making illiterate conversation and counting their pennies, you know in your heart they can't govern themselves. And they don't want to. They want full bellies, plenty of beer, a crummy little home that's all theirs, a couple of weeks on the Costa Notta Lotta every year, and a strong leader like Max who will do their thinking for them.

Pam: They don't want equality?

Samantha: Don't you lecture me about equality, Pam Jones. I've fought for equality.

Pam: You've what?

Samantha: I was the first girl ever to go to Eton, did you know that? The school said, she can't come here, she's a girl. But I was a feisty little girl, I said to them, my father's money is as good as any boy's father's money, and I made such a stink that they took me.

Pam: Have you ever lifted a finger for women whose parents can't afford Eton?

Samantha: Your lot never did a lot for them. If you had, maybe they wouldn't have turned to us.

Pam: You're playing a cruel trick on them. You say you'll put them first...

Samantha: And of course we can't. The wealth creators have to come first. Hopefully the poor will benefit in the end, but you can't expect them to understand that.

Pam: Maybe they're not so stupid as you think.

Samantha: I like you, Pam. You're a bright woman, and you're good company once you've had a bottle of Chablis to loosen you up. Go home to Michael, teach kids, do good in a small way if you must, but leave the country to us. It's us people want.

(*Pause.*)

Pam: You know all about Mrs M, I suppose?

Samantha: I'm afraid so.

Pam: Does it make any difference?

Samantha: You know, in Thailand you can live like a queen on the amount of money we send her. When did you find out?

Pam: Too late to use it in the election.

Samantha: Wouldn't have helped you. We'd have said you were persecuting her on racist grounds.

Pam: Likes them young, does he?

Samantha: Not always. He's a child himself really.

Pam: A dangerous child.

Samantha: Do you think the City can't bring him to heel when we need to?

(*Pause.*)

Pam: I'd like to go back to my cell now.

Samantha: Of course. You've got a lot to think about. There's someone waiting outside to take you. That door, please.

(*She points to a different door from the one the* KING *used. Exit* PAM.)

SCENE 10

Spot on MAX as he stands in the centre of the stage. He speaks in a new, heroic tone we have not heard before.

Max: They've burned our Parliament to the ground. But they cannot burn down the spirit of the British people.

While MPs gather in their new home in Stoke on Trent, here in London I am doing the business of the British people. And let the enemies of the people tremble.

I say to the men and women of the deep state who live in the shadows, to the liberal elites who demonstrate in the streets wherever they suspect the survival of a spirit of patriotism and decency, to the bureaucrats who take your taxes and hold back the wealth creators, I say to them: you are the enemies of the people.

No one can hide from the righteous wrath of the people. Even those closest to me can turn out to be enemies of the people – we have seen that today. I say to them: the British people are coming for you. We are going to drain the swamp.

The Deep State will not like it. The unions will strike. The House of Lords will try to sabotage us. The courts will see 'lawfare' and judicial activism. On our screens, outrage from mainstream media. In government departments, caviling and foot dragging. On the streets, protests.

But they speak for the old and crabbed. I speak for youth. For those young men who have been searching for a cause, and in the last few days have flocked to the aid of their country in its time of need.

They don't want Parliament, and elections, and wokery, and pronouns, and foreigners invading us like locusts, and LGBTQplus, whatever that is when it's at home.

They are done with those who think. Henceforth they will go with those who feel. They know what they feel, in their hearts, their sinews, their blood. They want passion and manhood and the pride of battle, and my God we are going to give it to them.

And if we have a prayer, as a great Christian nation must, it will be the prayer of that great Christian Englishman G.K. Chesterton:

> From sale and profanation
> Of honour and the sword
> From sleep and from damnation
> Deliver us good Lord.

SCENE 11

We are back in prison. Sounds of clanging doors, on screen a visual of prison bars. A bench. On it sit PAM and SAMANTHA, facing the audience.

Pam: I'm quite happy for you to take the lower bunk if you're more comfortable.

Samantha: Well, if you're sure....

Pam: We can talk properly here.

Samantha: You're sure? The last conversation we had in this room – well, that's why I'm here now.

Pam: The warder outside is in the union. He's "forgotten" to turn on the equipment. The union warders help us get messages out too.

Samantha: You mean there really is a leftwing conspiracy? I didn't make it up?

Pam: Yes. And now you're a part of it.

ENDS

.

www.ingramcontent.com/pod-product-compliance
Lightning Source LLC
Chambersburg PA
CBHW071008280626
47160CB00015B/2122